Starsky & Kered's Adventures

Karen Evans

Copyright © 2017 Karen Evans

All rights reserved, including the right to reproduce this book, or portions thereof in any form. No part of this text may be reproduced, transmitted, downloaded, decompiled, reverse engineered, or stored, in any form or introduced into any information storage and retrieval system, in any form or by any means, whether electronic or mechanical without the express written permission of the author.

This is a work of fiction. Names and characters are the product of the author's imagination and any resemblance to actual persons, living or dead, is entirely coincidental.

The views expressed in this work are solely those of the author and do not necessarily reflect the views of the publisher, and the publisher hereby disclaims any responsibility for them.

Front cover photo: Starsky & Kered waiting for a walk
Back photo: the author with Starsky & Kered,

ISBN: 978-0-244-01799-6

PublishNation
www.publishnation.co.uk

Starsky & Kered
Go to the Park

"Yawn" stretched Kered, forgetting momentarily where he was, waking from a lovely dream.

Looking around he smiled, remembering that he & Starsky are on holiday at Kaz & Andy's house in Leicester while Dave & Pat are away on their own holiday. Starsky is still fast asleep under the kitchen table, lying on his back with his legs in the air, Kered wondered how on earth that position could be comfy, but his companion always slept that way.

Getting up to stretch his legs, Kered wandered into the living and jumped up onto the settee knowing that Kaz wouldn't mind too much, she always pretended to be cross but deep down she wasn't. Kered loved spending time with Dave's daughter & her partner. His old companion Lucky had come to live with Kaz & Andy when she got to her twilight years, but was now no longer with us, Kered missed his old pal, but glad she had spent her last few years happy and well looked after.

Plodding down the stairs in her dressing gown, Kaz smiled and patted the poodles head affectionately as she went into the kitchen and switched the kettle on, hearing a noise, Starsky jumped up and banged his head on the kitchen table in his excitement "Who is it? Where am I?" he barked.

"Starsk, calm down" scolded Kaz, opening the back door so the dogs could go out and stretch their legs in the garden. Kaz's garden is a lot smaller than their own, but it suits Kaz & Andy and is perfect to stretch in. laughing at Starsky chasing a butterfly, Kaz sits down on the chair and drinks her coffee in the early morning sunshine, wondering what they could do today.

After getting dressed, Kaz calls the dogs, "Who fancies a trip to the park?" she asks, summersaulting around the garden in excitement Starsky knocks the chair over "Starsk!" chastises Kaz, picking the chair back up. Looking down his nose at his companion, Kered obediently sits and waits to be called to go for their walk.

Enjoying the new sights and smells on their walk, the dogs enjoyed the warmth from the sunshine, after a harsh winter, they are glad that spring was finally here and getting some warmth into their bones.

At the park, Kaz lets Starsky & Kered off their leads so they could run around, "STARSKY, KERED!" shouted a familiar voice, looking up, they saw their friend running towards them "BUSTER" they called in unison, Buster is a huge Chesapeake Retriever, who belongs to a friend of Kaz and loves cuddles, and like

Starsky, he also gets over excitable and loves people "I didn't know you were here yet, its fab to see you," laughed Buster summersaulting around the park with Starsky, as sensible as Kered is, he couldn't help but laugh at his friends antics. When the pair had calmed down, Kered asks Buster where his owner Jo was, "oh she is at work, but I'm here with Vicky & Jessica" responded Buster. Vicky is a friend of Jo, who walks Buster during the day while his owners are at work, Jessica is Vicky's three year old little girl, who Buster loves more than anything.

Looking up, Kered saw Jessica giggling at Starsky who was lying on his back hoping for a tummy tickle. Buster bounded over to them, not wanting to be left out of tummy tickles, "Come on!" Buster called to Kered, who smiled and walked over at a more sensible pace. Nudging Jessica's hand, Jessica put her arms around Kered for a cuddle and giggled into his neck. Smiling, Kered loved cuddles and knew that being the calmer dog, sometimes had its benefits.

Letting go, Jessica noticed the swings and asked her mummy to push her as high as she could, smiling, Kered wandered over to a big tree so he could lie in the shade, and watch Buster & Starsky bounding about having fun in the long grass.

Dozing off, Kered dreamed of butterflies and a big bone, when suddenly a noise woke him up, yawning

Kered Stretched and looked around wondering where his friends were, when he noticed a strange man approaching Jessica, feeling that something wasn't quite right, he looked around for Jessica's mummy who was talking to Kaz and laughing at Starsky & Buster doing summersaults around the field, bounding over to Jessica Kered balked as loudly as he could to get the others attention.

Kered sat at the little girls feet, and growled to warn the man, hearing the barking Starsky & Buster looked up and realised that Kered was protecting the child from a stranger, Nudging Kaz And Vicky's hands to alert them, they bounded over to them and sat around her in a protective circle until Vicky & Kaz reached them, picking Jessica up, Vicky asked "What are you doing all the way over here, munchkin?" "I wanted to pick some flowers for you mummy" smiled Jessica holding out some daisies for her mummy. Seeing the man carry on walking without looking back, Vicky hoped the man was just cutting through the park on his way somewhere, knowing that the park was a popular short cut route from the housing estate to the shops, but she was grateful to the dogs for protecting her child, patting them all on the head affectionately and giving them all a treat, knowing that the dogs would never hurt anybody, but would always protect those that are close to them.

A Trip to the Beach

"COMING" barked Starsky as Dave, his master calls him in for his breakfast. Starsky, An over exuberant blue border collie, comes skidding across the kitchen floor in his excitement for food, landing in a heap at his masters feet. "Slow down Starsk!" said his master affectionately as he pats the dog's head.

Kered, a well-bred black standard poodle looks on in disgust at Starsky's uncouthness as he quietly eats his breakfast, while Starsky bolts his down as quickly as he can. "I wish you'd train your dog proper manners" said Pat, Kered's mistress as she pats Kered's head and heads for the door to leave for work. "Bye have a good day" she calls as she picks up her car keys and leaves. Kered looks on forlornly. He wishes his mistress didn't have to leave him with Starsky on the days they both went out to work. He'd be far happier curled up in front of the aga in the kitchen instead of being stuck in a kennel outside. But the humans didn't like Starsky being in the house as he was known to raid the cupboards, no matter how dog proof they made them, so instead both dogs had to share a large heated kennel outside when the masters were out. It wasn't such a hardship, as they had duvets and a small old sofa in there, so it was more comfortable than most. "Come on then you two, I've decided to take the day off as it's such a nice day, who's up for a trip to the beach?" asked Dave, Starsky immediately started jumping about, knocking over the bin in excitement. Kered looked on with his nose in the air "ruffian" he sniffs.

Starsky's master opened the hatchback on his old 4X4 for the dogs to jump in, excitedly Starsky jumps up, Kered, sitting on the floor looks on in disgust, his mistress never puts him in the back when she takes him out, she always lets him have the backseat, "come on Kered, in" Called Dave, "oh I get it, you want to go on the backseat" he says realising why Kered was so reluctant to get in, seeing Starsky still jumping about, he opens the door to the backseat for Kered, Kered is definitely the better behaved of the two dogs, but Starsky had such a tough background, he finds it hard to discipline him properly, and he is so loyal, never leaving his masters side. "I guess it won't hurt just this once, up you go boy" wagging his tail Kered jumped up onto the backseat and immediately lies down.

Kered loves long walks either to the beach or on the moors, Pat took him for several walks at the beach just the two of them before she met Starsky and his master, it's not that Kered doesn't like Starsky, it's just that they have completely different backgrounds, Starsky was a rescue dog, having no idea what happened to him before he was rescued, where

Kered has always lived with his mistress, having been well looked after, and spoilt all his life, so suddenly having to share it with the over excitable collie has been hard to adjust to. But he has to hand it to Starsky, he is incredibly loyal to his master, he just wished he wasn't so excitable about everything, sometimes he missed his quiet life when it was just him and his mistress.

When they got to the beach, both dogs jumped out, Starsky jumping about in circles like he was about to explode with excitement. Kered sat obediently waiting for Dave to lock the car and give the command to walk. Kered knew that Starkey's master didn't favour him as much as his own dog, often referring to him as a wuss, which hurt his feelings but his mistress often defended him and he knew she loved him, Kered went to live with her not long after she was widowed and spent all her spare time teaching him obedience and agility and sometimes he went with her to work at the pet shop and he loves sitting in the shop keeping guard and being made a fuss of by the customers.

"Come on then both of you" called Starsky's master giving the command to walk, Starsky, who was sniffing enthusiastically at a small patch of grass bounded over almost skidding to a halt at his masters feet. Kered put his nose in the air with disgust at Starsky's bullishness. Starsky leapt and jumped about in excitement running in front, then stopping waiting for them to catch up then running in front again, sniffing at strange objects on the sand, trying to eat a piece of seaweed then spitting it back out almost immediately as it tasted horrible, there was nobody else on the beach, and it felt like both dogs owned the stretch of sand before them, they were free to run and roam as they pleased, Kered loved the feel of the sand beneath his paws, and as they walked towards the sea edge, he loved to paddle and get his feet wet. When Dave got two tennis balls out of his pocket, Kered looked on excitedly, as obedient as he was, he loved to chase balls and would often play dirty by pulling Starsky's tail if he thought Starsky was going to get to the ball first. So usually Starsky would let Kered go off in front to let him think he'd get the ball first, then speed up and overtake and get to the ball just at the last second, it was a game both dogs enjoyed playing and would play ball all day if their masters would let them. After a good game of ball, Starsky's master decided to sit on a large rock to rest and poured some water from a bottle into a bowl for the dogs while he opened a can of pop for himself, Starsky's excitement hadn't ebbed and in his excitement to get to the water bowl he stood in it and tipped the bowl over, "Starsk, careful" his owner chastised. Kered put his nose in the air "peasant" he grumbled. Pouring another bowl of water for the dogs, Starsky greedily lapped up the water. Kered hated sharing a water bowl with the other dog but knew he had no choice as he was so thirsty after all the running around chasing the balls.

After a good drink, Starsky became agitated, looking up, Kered realised that something was seriously wrong with Dave. The colour of his face was odd, and the expression on his face was pained. Panicking, the dogs barked and barked, but as nobody else was on the beach nobody heard, starting to worry Kered didn't know what to do, Starsky, started to nudge his owners hand to let him know he was there, and barked at Kered to run and get help. Kered ran in the direction of the car park, but that was at least two miles away, but he ran as fast as he could leaving Starsky comforting his master. When he finally got back to the car, seeing there were no other cars round, he started to cry not knowing what to do. After five minutes, he heard a voice "here boy what's up, come on its okay" Kered looked round and saw a kind looking man crouching down and calling to him, "where's your master boy?" the man asked. Barking, Kered ran off in the direction of the beach a few paces, stopped, looked back round to the man and ran again towards the beach hoping the man would follow. Confused the man decided to follow the dog a few paces to see if he could see where the owner of the dog could be, Kered continued the process of barking, running a few paces and stopping in attempt to get the man to follow.

When Kered got back to where Starsky and his master were, the master was now lying down and Starsky was lying next to him looking sad. Fortunately the kind looking man had followed Kered, and when he saw the man on the ground, he immediately called for an ambulance and went straight to the man to put him into the recovery position. Thinking what amazing dogs they were to be able to get help. The kind man checked the collars of both dogs to get a telephone number so that he could call home. Just as he was about to make a call the ambulance arrived. Starsky didn't want to leave his master and immediately started pinning when the door to the ambulance shut with the dogs on the outside. "Sorry boy no pets allowed" said the paramedic towards the dogs, not knowing what to do, the man called the mobile number that was on Kered's collar. Not wanting to worry the lady that answered, he asked if she was the owner of a black poodle and a collie, concerned she asked why. So he explained that he was with the dogs on the beach and that Starsky's master had been taken ill. With two dogs looking so forlorn, he knew he couldn't abandon them.

A few days later, Starsky's owner was out of hospital after having had a minor heart attack at the beach, Starsky was over the moon at his master's return home and went to greet him in his usual over exuberant way, having missed his master so much he knocked everything over in his excitement. "Down Starsk" said his master affectionately, even Kered was excited at having Starsky's master home, went to greet his arrival. Patting Kered's head affectionately, he knew he owed the dogs a lot for getting help when he fell ill on their walk. Wondering who the kind person was that took care of the dogs when it happened, nobody seemed to know who the man was, or where he came from, he disappeared as quickly as he arrived. The following day, the local press had reported sightings of ghostly happenings in the area, a local sketch artist had put together some pictures that he had drawn based on the reports from people. "Look at this" called Pat, over her morning coffee, the pictures looked uncannily like their mystery man, who had been named as a local man who died many years ago while on an animal rights campaign. A cold shiver ran through both owners.

Samuel Comes to Visit

"Yawn" stretches Kered waking up from a restful sleep. He smiled as he stretched; knowing that today was the day that Samuel, his owner's three year old grandson was coming to stay for a few days.

Samuel lived in Sheffield with his mummy & Daddy so doesn't come to visit very often, as it is very far from Cornwall where Kered lives with his owners, Pat & Dave and his companion, Starsky.

Glancing over at Starsky, Kered smiled to himself, even when asleep Starsky can't keep quiet or still – in the midst of a dream Starsky yelps and grumbles, his front paws flailing madly as though he is chasing after something and barking at whatever it is to slow down.

Noticing that the back door is slightly ajar, Kered nudges the door open with his nose and goes over to the patio table where Pat is sitting reading the paper and drinking her morning mug of tea. "Hello, boy" smiles Pat, noticing the poodle coming towards her. Kered sits by her feet and rests his head on her lap, he loves the alone time with just him and his mistress. As much as he loves Starsky, he does miss the quietness that he once knew before Pat had met Dave and Starsky.

Suddenly the back door burst open, and out bounded Starsky, somersaulting across the yard. "Where is he? Is he here yet? Why didn't you wake me!!?"

"Calm down Starsk!!" chastised Pat standing up and getting the tennis balls from the cupboard. "I Think you pair need a good run before Samuel gets here" she muttered going over to the exercise field. Obediently Kered followed his mistress, while Starsky cartwheeled all the way over to the field, unable to curtain his excitement. "Peasant!" sniffed Kered putting his nose in the air.

While the dogs were having fun chasing the balls, each other & stray blossom that was falling from the trees, Starsky noticed a car pulling up in the drive. "They're here" he barked excitedly bounding over in the direction of the car. "Starsky, HERE" called Pat, worried that the over excitable Collie would jump up at the car and knock something or somebody over.

"Down boy" laughs Jay getting out of the car. Obediently both dogs sit down, as excitable as Starsky is; he knows that in his excitement his size could easily knock the toddler over and cause distress, so used all of his effort to keep calm.

"Hi guys, good trip?" asked Pat hugging Jay & Lisa as they got out the car and unclipped Samuel from his car seat.

"Hiya Pat" shouted Samuel running to his Nanny Pat for a cuddle, making everybody smile at his enthusiasm "Hiya Samuel" laughed Pat picking him up for a big hug & kiss.

"Your dad has just gone shop to get something for dinner, he shouldn't be too long" Pat said to Jay, putting Samuel down so that he could run around in the late morning sunshine.

Starsky & Kered followed Samuel around, keeping an eye on him while he played. "Woof, woof" laughed Samuel when he realised that the dogs were nearby.

Jay & Lisa emptied the car while Pat made coffee and got some biscuits out the cupboard, stretching Lisa pulled a chair into the sunshine so she could get some warmth into her back and also keep an eye on Samuel.

"Dave's taking his time at the shop" exclaimed Pat bringing the coffee & biscuits outside "he's no doubt found somebody to talk to and lost track of time" she thought, picking up her phone to call him to let him know that his grandson was here.

Suddenly they heard a car at the top of the lane, recognising the sound Starsky ran around barking, forgetting momentarily about Samuel, Kered managed to get in between Starsky & Samuel just as Starsky Jumped up in his excitement almost sending the toddler flying, with a quick yelp Kered took the brunt and glared at his companion to calm down – it's not as though Dave had been gone THAT long! Giggling at the commotion, Samuel followed the dogs to see who the car belonged to "Grandad" he called when he saw who was getting out the car "hiya Grandad" he shouted running to greet his grandad "Hiya Samuel" laughed Dave picking his Grandson up and swinging him around "blimey when did you get so big!" he exclaimed, amazed at how big the little boy had got in such a short space of time. Even though Dave & Pat talk on FaceTime most weeks with Jay, Lisa & Samuel, it's not the same as actually being with them and felt sad that he's missing out on a lot of the growing up, but was determined that they were going to make the most of this visit

"Starsky, down" shouted Pat at the over excitable dog, who just couldn't contain his excitement at having visitors and was doing cartwheels around the yard. Sitting with his nose in the air, Kered was preening at the attention Lisa was giving him, he loved the extra attention that he got from Samuel's mummy and was often sad when she had gone home. "STARSKY! That's enough, INSIDE, now, both of you!" yelled Pat, worried that Starsky would crash into Samuel and hurt him, knowing that it wasn't fair to punish Kered as well, but she knew Starsky would only whine if he had to go in while Kered stayed outside.

Glaring at his companion, Kered obediently went inside and sat in his basket while Starsky carried on doing cartwheels until he got to the door and went into his bed. "Ruffian" grumbled Kered, sitting with his back to the collie, clearly not happy that he has had to go inside too.

Lying down on their beds, Starsky quickly fell back to sleep, snoring and fidgeting while he dreamt, Kered, laying with his head between his paws listening to the family outside talking and hearing Samuel laughing soon made the Poodle smile again, he knew he couldn't be cross with the collie for long, as he couldn't help the way that he was, but thought of the unfairness of being punished when he hadn't done anything wrong himself.

Feeling quite tired Kered decided to make use of the quiet time and have a nap as well.

Suddenly the back door flung open, and Starsky & Kered sat up wondering what was happening, sensing Pat's distress, Kered went straight to his owner and nudged her hand. Starsky, hearing a sob come from outside and went to investigate and saw Lisa sitting with a limp Samuel on her lap, Keen to not let Kered see Samuel like this decided to nudge the back door shut so Kered couldn't come out.

Not knowing what had happened, but hearing Dave's frantic voice shouting into his phone, Starsky knew he had to do something. Giving Lisa & Samuel a gentle kiss each to let them know he was there, the dog then ran as fast as he could to a neighbour's farm half a mile away, hoping they would be in.

He arrived just as they were getting into their car, barking as loudly as he could to get their attention Starsky ran over to the car hoping they would see him in time. "Hello Starsk, what brings you here?" said Pete, a retired doctor. Continuing to bark, Starsky ran towards the road and stopped and looked round hoping that Pete would follow. Wondering what had got into the dog, Pete ran after the dog to make sure he was ok. When they got back home, Samuel was sitting up but looking very subdued.

"Pete!" Called Dave. Relived that Samuel was sitting up, Starsky went over to the little boy and kissed his hand and sat down, "what happened?" queried the neighbour, realising that something was wrong with the child.

"We're not sure" sobbed Lisa, "he was playing over there, when he fell and banged his head" noticing a bruise appear on the child, Pete shone a light into Samuel's eyes to check his pupils and checked his temperature and pulse, happy that he seemed fine he put his hand in his pocket and gave the child a sweet for being brave.

"Doggy" said Samuel giggling at Starsky who was sitting up on his back legs, as he knew this always made the child laugh "he'll be fine" said Pete laughing at the dogs antics, "We tried calling you" said Dave, "obviously Starsky had the same idea" he exclaimed, amazed at how the dog knew who to fetch.

The back door opened and out came Pat with Kered, bringing strong sweet tea for the grown-ups and juice for Samuel, relieved that he appeared to have recovered from his accident.

Kered went to Lisa, knowing he would be able to comfort her, even though Samuel was now fine after his fall, he knew Lisa would still be in shock.

Putting her arms round Kered for a cuddle, Lisa smiled wondering how the dogs can be so sensitive to their feelings.

Keeping an eye on Samuel, who was happily playing in the field with Starsky, she knew that this bump would probably be the first of many, and hoped that Starsky & Kered would be there to love & protect the child as much as they could while he grows up.

Starsky & Kered with their friends Cheeky & Lucky

A DAY AT THE BEACH

"Wake up, wake up" barked Starsky excitedly. "What time IS it?" yawned Kered sleepily. "Time to get up, lazy bones" barked Starsky excitedly. "We're going to the beach today, remember? It's a warm spring day, ideal for paddling in the sea". Starsky is an over excitable Border collie. Kered, a black standard poodle, stretches, yawns, and looks at the clock. "But it's only 8 O'clock" he grumbles as he heads for the bathroom to wash his face and brush his teeth.

Starsky wandered down to the kitchen to finish packing the picnic basket with all sorts of nice food. Kered is health conscious and favours fruit and salad rather than crisps and sweets, so Starsky packed a good mix of fruit and salad with a few sweets and biscuits as a treat. When Kered had finished in the bathroom and had dressed, he went downstairs for breakfast. Starsky had poured cereal into the bowls but had spilled quite a bit over the work top, as well as there being more jam on the table than there was on the toast. "Starsky just look at all this mess" chastised Kered, but he couldn't be cross at the collie for long as he knew that he was only trying to help and couldn't help his exuberance. "I Think I'll pour the tea" Kered said, trying to sound cross, but couldn't help smiling at the collie who had managed to get jam all over his face.

Once the dogs had finished breakfast and had cleaned up, they were ready to go. Starsky couldn't contain his excitement; he loved the beach, the feel of the sand between his paws, the cool sea to paddle in, as well as the freedom of being able to run for miles with no traffic to worry about.

The beach wasn't as busy as Kered expected it to be, so they found a sheltered area by some rocks and unpacked a blanket to sit on and the toys to play with. Both dogs loved to chase balls and Frisbee with a passion. "Let's play, please Kered, please, please" barked Starsky, jumping about in excitement as though he were about to burst. "Wait, have a drink first" Kered said unpacking the water and a bowl. Kered also loved the beach and the freedom it gave, but was well mannered enough to contain his excitement. After a good drink, the dogs decided to play Frisbee. "Put your cap and some sunscreen on first" called Kered. Even though it was breezy; Kered knew that the sun was powerful enough to still burn. "You're such a spoilsport" grumbled Starsky as he reluctantly protected himself from the sun's harmful rays.

The dogs could see nobody else at all on the beach and soon started chasing the Frisbee and each other, barking and laughing and having fun in the sunshine. After several hours of playing, the dogs decided to head back to their belongings so they could eat their picnic. To cool down, they wandered along the sea edge to paddle in the sea. Starsky is a long haired collie and loves to get completely wet to cool off. Kered isn't as confident in the water as his companion, but has fun watching Starsky splashing about and couldn't help but laugh when a big wave caught Starsky by surprise and enveloped him. Being a strong swimmer, Starsky swam out spluttering and laughing. "Let's go get some food" laughed Kered "so you can dry off". Laughing, Starsky shook himself and they walked back to their belongings in companionable silence.

"Where's our food?" queried Kered when they returned to the blanket. "We left the basket right here" Said Starsky. "Our toys have gone too" he said forlornly. Not sure what to do, the dogs sat on the blanket so they could decide on a plan of action. "We have to tell the police" Said Kered. Hot and upset, the dogs folded the blanket and walked towards the road so that they could tell the police of the theft. After a few minutes, Starsky spotted something move from the corner of his eye, turning, he saw what looked to be their picnic basket moving by itself. "Kered, look!" Starsky barked in astonishment. Looking towards where Starsky was pointing, Kered saw the picnic basket disappear behind some rocks. "Come on, lets follow it" barked Kered running towards the rocks.

When the dogs got there, they saw a straggly looking dog helping himself to their food. "Who are you?" asked Kered and Starsky at the same time. The dog looked up startled, and then looked down sadly. "Please don't be cross, I am very sorry, I'm just so hungry" said the dog forlornly. "What's your name?" asked Starsky. "I don't know, I've never had a proper home, so I find food and shelter where I can" said the stray dog quietly. "I spend a lot of time down here at the beach as the picnics I find are easy pickings". "You do know that it's wrong and against the law to take what isn't yours?" said Kered crossly. "Please don't be mad at me, I'm just so hungry, and your food was just so tempting, I really couldn't help myself". The dog said sadly. "Look, I'm hungry too, and there's more than enough food here for the three of us, so let's eat while we decide what to do next" said Starsky. Kered put his nose in the air, not liking the situation or Starsky's suggestion at sharing their food with this stray, but kept quiet. Starsky knows what it's like to be homeless; being a rescued dog himself, so has an empathy for waifs and strays.

After eating all the food in the basket in silence, the three dogs laid down in the sun. "We should give you a name" Starsky said. The scruffy dog was painfully thin, and a cross between a collie and a spaniel, having long spaniel ears but with the build of a border collie, with short straggly fur. "I think Scruff or Tramp would suit him" sniffed Kered with his nose in the air. "Ignore my friend, he's such a snob" said Starsky glaring at Kered for being so rude. "Don't worry, its fine" said the stray "actually I like Tramp, it fits well doesn't it?" he smiled. Laughing Starsky said "well Tramp it is then, pleased to meet you, I'm Starsky, and this here is Kered".

"How long have you been living at the beach?" asked Kered. "A few months" Tramp then told them the story of his abandonment, being dumped from a car near to the beach at just a few months old, and having to fend for himself since. Tramp looked so sad and lonely that both Kered and Starsky felt sorry for him. Starsky in particular knows all about abandonment as his owners didn't want him either and ended up in the local dogs home for a long while until he was rescued by Kered's owners. "Thank you for sharing your picnic with me, I'll never forget your kindness, but I'd better not hold you up any longer" said Tramp as he got up to go. "Wait, where will you go?" asked Kered "It's not safe being here by yourself at night" said Starsky. "Thank you for your concern, but I'm careful and I'll be fine, please don't worry" Tramp said as he heads for the rocks where he shelters at night.

"Come on Starsky lets go home" said Kered packing their rubbish and toys back into the basket. "But we can't just leave Tramp" pleaded Starsky. "Well he can't come home with us can he, where will he sleep". Realising that the subject was closed, Starsky reluctantly followed his companion home.

A few days later, Starsky couldn't help but wonder about the dog they had met on their trip to the beach, and thought about Tramp daily. Kered refused to even talk about him. But there was something about Tramp that bothered Starsky, but he couldn't understand why. He'd asked Kered several times if they could go back to the beach to take some food for the stray but Kered had said a firm no.

But Starsky couldn't help thinking that there should be something he could do to help, after all, Tramp couldn't help being homeless, and with winter not far away, he felt he needed to do something. The next day, Sharon, a relative, called round for a visit. The two dogs always enjoyed Sharon's visits as she always has plenty of fuss and treats for them. This time she also brought her son, Matthew, who is profoundly deaf. Matthew has always been shy around the dogs so they are always extra gentle with him, sitting still and placing their heads near to his hand or on his knee for fuss, Matthew isn't keen on sudden movements and often gets upset if the dogs jump up or get excitable.

While the dogs were enjoying being fussed by Matthew, Sharon and Pat, Kered's owner, were talking about getting an assistance dog for Matthew to help him gain confidence and independence in the world. "I love the idea" said Sharon, "but you know how shy he is with dogs. We'd have to get one so docile that wouldn't get spooked by Matthew's outbursts, and wouldn't upset Matthew with sudden movements, as well as being able to assist Matthew with everyday life". "Yes, but if you get a dog young enough to train to assist Matthew, plus, dogs pick up on peoples moods, just look how Starsky and Kered are with him" Said Pat affectionately. "And we can train the dog to help Matthew". Pat used to train dogs when she was much younger, both for obedience and agility.

Listening intently to the conversation going on, Starsky was thinking about Tramp, and how he'd be perfect as an assistance dog for Matthew. But Kered, who knew exactly what Starsky was thinking, glared at his companion and shook his head in disagreement. Lying down, Starsky put his head between his paws looking forlorn, as he knew that convincing Kered would be hard work. "What's up with you, Starsk?" Queried Sharon stroking his head. Starsky immediately rolled onto his back, hoping Sharon would tickle his tummy, laughing Matthew and Sharon both tickled him. "Starsky, what you like, any excuse for a tummy tickle" Sharon laughed.

After Sharon and Matthew had gone home, Kered and Starsky sat in the garden watching the sky. "I know what you're thinking and no! We can't bring Tramp home" Kered scolded Starsky. "But why?" asked the collie. "Because we don't know anything about him, that's why." Kered grumbled. "But you didn't know anything about me when I first came to live here, but we're now good friends. Aren't we?" Starsky tried to reason. "That's different. You were a companion for me, we don't know if Tramp is ok with children. Plus he's used to his own company, we don't know how he'd cope being with Matthew all day every day".

"When you're an abandoned dog, all you want is company and would do anything to get that company, and will love having somebody there all the time. Plus, he will have us to help out and play with, won't he?" Starsky reasoned. But Kered was no longer listening, having dozed off. Sharon and Matthew only lived nearby, so called in most days. All Starsky had to do was try and get Tramp to follow them back from the beach, and hope that Sharon falls for him.

The next day, Starsky and Kered decided to go for a walk. "Please can we go to the beach and see Tramp? Please, please?" pleaded Starsky. "Okay, we'll go" Kered reluctantly said. He knew that Starsky would never shut up about it if they didn't go back. "We might not even find him, though, so don't get your hopes up". Jumping about, Starsky was so happy that

Kered had finally given in. He packed some food and toys to take with them.

It was a lovely warm day and the dogs enjoyed a leisurely stroll to the beach, Starsky loved to chase the birds off that were feasting on left over scraps that people had carelessly left behind. They found Tramps hiding place straight away and went to look for him. "He's not here" commented Kered, "but look, there's a blanket over in that corner, so he has been here recently" said Starsky excitedly. "I wonder where he could be?" Starsky wondered. "Well he's not here, he may be looking for food" answered Kered. "Let's leave our things here, they should be safe and go and play Frisbee, while the beach is so quiet".

After several hours of playing chase and paddling in the sea, Starsky and Kered decide to walk back to their belongings as they were both becoming tired and hungry. Deciding to go for a swim to cool off Starsky headed to the sea. Kered just paddled along the edge, preferring to just get his paws wet instead of going in completely. He wished he had his partner's confidence with water but he was happy to watch Starsky splashing about and getting enveloped by the waves. Starsky is a strong swimmer and always swims out of them laughing and spluttering. By the time they got back to their belongings, they saw a dog sitting by their picnic basket excitedly wagging a tail. "Tramp" barked Starsky excitedly running and jumping over to the dog. Tramp excitedly ran towards to the two dogs "I was hoping it would be you" he barked excitedly. The three dogs greeted each other with excitement. "We've brought food" Said Starsky, "please say you'll eat with us?" Starsky asked the stray. "Well, only if it's ok with both of you" Tramp asked, looking at Kered. "Of course its ok" smiled Kered. "Besides, we have something to ask you" Kered said. Looking astonished, Starsky turned to his companion and said "You mean it's ok? I can ask him?" "Ask me what? Asked Tramp, intrigued. "Well how would you like a home to live in and be looked after, like us?" grinned Starsky. "Really? With you guys? That'd be great" Tramp jumped about excitedly. "Not quite with us" Kered explained about Sharon and Matthew. "But don't get your hopes up, they might not even want to keep you" warned Kered. "I'll be good, honest, I'll try my best" said Tramp, feeling the happiest he had for a long time. "But first we need to get you cleaned up" Kered said with his nose in the air. Laughing Starsky and Tramp did a high five.

After eating their picnic and dozing in the sun, Kered started packing up the basket. "Can you swim?" Starsky asked Tramp. "I love the water" Tramp answered, "that's a good idea" exclaimed Kered, "why don't you two go and have a quick swim and hopefully Tramp will look a bit more presentable". Laughing Tramp and Starsky ran towards the sea while Kered finished packing their belongings. The two dogs had fun splashing about in the water for a few minutes before heading back to where Kered was waiting. "That's better" laughed Kered looking at Tramp who no longer looked so dirty. "Hopefully Sharon will still be at the house and we can introduce you to her, but remember, no jumping up or she'll never agree to have you" warned Kered. "Okay" answered Tramp, happy but nervous at the same time. What if Sharon or Matthew didn't like him? This was his one chance to have a loving home; he hoped he didn't mess it up.

When they walked up the drive they saw Sharon, Pat and Matthew standing by Sharon's car. "Here they are" smiled Sharon greeting the dogs, "we wondered where you had gone" she smiled affectionately at them. "Who's this then?" she said to Tramp. Tramp immediately sat down and hung his head low, not sure how to react. Starsky and Kered looked at each other worriedly, hoping Sharon would like him. "It's ok boy, come" said Sharon, kneeling down and calling Tramp to her. Tramp went straight to her, licked her hand and sat down wagging his tail. "You're a nice looking dog, where have you come from then?" Sharon said to Tramp making a fuss of him, "He has no collar on, I wonder if he's a stray" Sharon said looking at Pat. "He's very thin too" Pat exclaimed also stroking Tramp. Tramp laid down enjoying the attention, but remembered what his friends had said about not getting too excited, it was important he remained calm, despite wanting to jump about with excitement. "Let's take him into the yard and feed him and make a few phone calls, to see if he's been reported as lost or missing" Sharon said. Wagging their tails enthusiastically all three dogs followed Sharon and Pat into the yard. Noticing Matthew watching the new dog shyly, Tramp gently nudged Matthew's hand. Giggling Matthew timidly stroked the new dogs head. Looking round to see what Matthew was laughing at, Sharon looked surprised as Matthew, who is normally so timid with dogs he didn't know, was tickling the stray's tummy, while the stray was wagging his tail enthusiastically. Starsky and Kered also looked on with surprise at seeing Matthew so relaxed with their new friend. Starsky smiled to himself, pleased that Tramp had made such an impression on the child, and secretly hoped that Sharon would want to keep him as an assistance dog for Matthew.

Several phone calls later, Pat found that no dogs matching Tramps description had been reported missing. "What are we going to do with him?" Sharon exclaimed. "He's so thin; he obviously hasn't been looked after properly".

"Well, I haven't got room for him, not with this pair" Pat said, looking at Starsky and Kered with affection. "Besides, he might have owners, who just haven't got round to reporting him missing yet?" Pat said, thinking aloud. "But just look at how thin he is, whoever owns him obviously hasn't fed him properly. The police have my details and said they'd call if anybody does report him missing, but my guess is he's a stray" said Sharon. Stroking Tramp's ear. Listening in on the conversation, all three dogs look on forlornly, hoping that Sharon will keep the stray.

"So, what ARE we going to do with him?" Sharon asks again. She's tempted to keep him for herself, especially after seeing how Matthew was with him. "Sharon, I hope you're not thinking what I think you're thinking!" Pat scolded, seeing the look on Sharon's face. "We should take him to the dogs' home" Pat said. "Well you saw how Matthew was with him, when has Matthew ever been like that with dogs he doesn't know?" Sharon queried.

Deciding to sleep on it, Pat reluctantly agrees to let Tramp sleep with Starsky and Kered, and Sharon promised to take Tramp to the vets the following day for a check-up. All three dogs jump about in excitement at this news, knowing that Sharon had already fallen for the stray.

The following day, Sharon arrives bright and early for Tramp. Matthew's face lit up when he saw the stray. Stretching, Tramp plodded over to Matthew, sat down and Matthew affectionately tickled his ears, laughing. Tramp can't remember the last time he felt so happy and wanted, and really hoped Sharon would agree to give him a home. In the car on the way to the vet, Matthew sat in the back, and Tramp rested his head on Matthew's leg, contented.

Back at home, Starsky and Kered wouldnt settle, worried that Sharon may take their friend to the dogs home instead of taking him home, aware that Pat isn't keen on the dog. Noticing that the dogs are restless, Pat takes them for a good walk on Dartmoor, which they love, chasing balls and each other, they momentarily forget how their friend may be getting on.

Several hours later, as Pats car pull into the drive, they notice Sharon's car is also in the drive. Barking and jumping about, Kered and Starsky hope that Sharon hasn't taken Tramp to the dogs home. Jumping out of the car, they notice Tramp and Matthew playing in the field, so they run over to join in the fun. Kered notices a bright red collar around Tramp's neck, "Guess what?" barked Tramp excitedly. "Sharon has decided to keep me for Matthew" Tramp jumped about, unable to contain his excitement, "I finally have a loving home". All three dogs jump about in excitement, with Matthew looking on laughing. "The best thing is" barks Tramp, "is that Sharon also decided to call me Tramp". All three dogs fall about in laughter.

VISITORS

"They must be expecting visitors" grumbled Kered and Starsky almost at the same time. Their owners were having a mad spring clean of the house, while the dogs were banished to the garden to play, which wasn't so bad as it was a warm autumnal day and the neighbours red setter, Ruby, was also out. The three dogs often liked to run up and down along the fence which separated the two gardens.

It's not that they resented having visitors, as the two dogs were often spoilt with extra fuss, treats and long walks - depending on who it was visiting. It was just the disruption to their normal every day routine which the dogs resented.

After several hours of playing chase and sniffing and generally enjoying the unusually warm October sunshine, a car pulled into the driveway. "It's THEM" barked Starsky so excitedly he somersaulted down the driveway in a rush to greet his visitors. "Ruffian" sniffed Kered. As excited as Kered was at seeing who the visitor was, he was well mannered enough to not disgrace himself by doing cartwheels down the drive to greet them.

When the car pulled to a halt, an over excited Starsky ran round the car, not sure who would step out the car first. "How's my boys," said Kaz excitedly, making a fuss of the two dogs, while Andy let Lucky, their elderly black and white collie, out of the car, wagging her tail in excitement at visiting her former home and seeing the two dogs again.

Lucky went to live with Kaz and Andy recently so that she could enjoy her twilight years in peace. As much as she loved and missed Starsky and Kered, she did enjoy, and loved being the only dog in the house and getting sole attention from her new owners. Also she knew she'd get to visit her former home regularly. So she had the best of both worlds.

"LUCKY" barked Starsky and Kered excitedly. Sniffing round her, pleased she had come for a visit. After a long car journey, Lucky was starting to feel her age and was glad to be able stretch her legs. "Okay then you lot, let's go" called Kaz, aware that the dogs needed a run to get some of the excitement out of their system, and took the dogs to their exercise field. Despite her age, Lucky loved long walks and had a passion for chasing balls. She wasn't as quick as the younger dogs, but she gave them a good run for their money and occasionally the younger dogs would let her get to the ball first out of respect for her age.

After a few minutes of ball chasing they headed towards the house. Still excitable at who the visitor was, Starsky bounded into the kitchen for a drink, knocking over the bin at the same time. "Starsky, careful" called Dave, his master, attempting to sound angry, but he couldn't be mad at the loveable dog, no matter how hard he tried. "Hi guys good journey?" he asked his only daughter and son in law greeting them with hugs. "How's Lucky?" he enquired, pleased to see his old dog looking so well, she wagged her tail enthusiastically in return. He knew Lucky would be happy going to live with Kaz, she loved dogs and had missed not having one of her own, so when he suggested she take on Lucky, she jumped at the chance. "How's you dad? I hope you're taking things easy after your recent scare". Her dad had had a minor heart attack recently while out with the dogs, and had been advised by his doctor to take things easy, but she knew his active lifestyle is what kept him going. "You know your dad, Kaz, he'll never slow down" said Pat, Kered's owner, walking into the kitchen to greet the visitors. "Hey Lucky's looking great" she observed, pleased that Lucky seemed to have settled into her new home. Aware that she was being talked about, Lucky wagged her tail enthusiastically and nudged Pat's hand for fuss.

Putting the dogs outside to play, their owners went into the living room with tea and biscuits to catch up. "So, what are your plans while you're here?" enquired Dave. "Oh you know, walk the dogs and not a lot else" grinned Kaz. Kaz and Andy lived in a big town in the

Midlands, while her dad lived in the middle of nowhere in Cornwall, so they loved getting out and walking the dogs on nearby Dartmoor or along the beach when it was out of season.

"Well we'd better unload the car before it gets dark" Andy said getting up. Following him, Kaz asked her dad which room they'd be in. "The usual one" he informed her, taking the mugs and biscuit tin off his daughter and heading for the kitchen. All three dogs heard the back door open and went running up to Andy in excitement, "no, not another walk, we'll go out tomorrow" he told them affectionately. Knowing the dogs wouldn't be disheartened for long, he headed to the car to get the bags.

When Andy had taken the bags out of the car, he looked up to close the boot, and saw a figure of a person in the distance, over in the second field which hardly gets used. Andy thought nothing of it as he knew Pat was thinking of renting out one of her fields, so assumed it must have been the new owner. Walking back to the house with the bags, Starsky started jumping about excitedly, Kaz and Andy never came for a visit without bringing treats, "down Starsk" chastised Andy, taking the bags indoors. Lucky and Kered were dozing in front of the open fire, even though Kered is a much younger dog, he missed Lucky immensely when she went to live with Kaz. He never left her side and enjoyed her company whenever they came for visits. After taking the bags upstairs, Kaz called in Starsky to give the dogs the chews she had brought down. Excitedly, Starsky bowled in like a whirlwind, knocking over anything in his way. Lucky and Kered put their noses up in disgust. "Adolescent" sniffed Lucky, forgetting that Kered is of similar age to Starsky. Lucky enjoyed Kered's company and she often felt guilty for leaving him with the over exuberant collie, but now that she's elderly, she is far happier being the only dog in a household that loved her immensely, and not having to share the fire, treats or her owners affections. Gently taking the chews, Kered and Lucky settled back in front of the fire, while Starsky took his as far away from the others as he could, something he's always done with food.

"Who have you rented the back field out to?" Andy asked Pat over dinner. Exchanging glances, Dave shifted uncomfortably in his seat, "Nobody as yet," answered Pat. "I haven't done anything about it to be honest, as Sharon is keen to start doing agility again and would like to use that field". Sharon is Pat's daughter who lives nearby. "Why'd you ask?" enquired Pat, "Oh no reason," shrugged Andy, thinking that the light and tiredness must have been playing tricks on his eyes.

The following day, Kaz and Andy decided to take the dogs to Dartmoor for a long walk. Opening up the back of Dave's old 4 x 4, Starsky and Lucky immediately jumped in the back. Kered disliked sharing the back with Starsky, but reluctantly jumped in so he could be close to Lucky. Once the dogs realised where they were going, Starsky started jumping about with excitement. Lucky and Kered exchanged disgusted glances at the collie's over enthusiastic behaviour. As happy as they were to be taken to the moor for a walk, they were well mannered enough to contain their excitement. Letting the dogs out, Kaz put the leads in her pocket just in case. She's never needed the leads on a walk, but she always carried them anyway. Locking up the car, Andy puts the keys in his pocket and called the dogs and walked towards the river. Knowing how much Lucky loves the water, but doesn't get the chance back home to play in it. Starsky and Lucky immediately jump in splashing about, and chasing sticks. Kered isn't so keen and prefers to sniff by the side and stick close to Kaz. As much as Kered loves to be close to Lucky, he has a fear of water and will just get close enough to the edge to drink but doesn't like to go in. after a few minutes of playing, Kaz and Andy call the dogs to continue the walk and to let them dry off. Several hours later, they head home. Parking the car, Andy goes to the back of the car to let the dogs out, looking up, he sees the same figure in the back field that he'd seen the day before. "Do you see that?" he asks Kaz. "It's probably just Dad or Pat" shrugs Kaz walking towards the house. Opening the back door, Dave and Pat were sat in the kitchen drinking tea and talking. "Good walk?" they both asked almost at the same time, "yeah it was good" said Kaz "we walked for miles". "I've left the dogs outside as they're filthy" said Andy, walking in behind Kaz. "I'll hose them down in a bit" smiled Dave, knowing how much the dogs loved to get as dirty as possible on walks. "Do it now before the dogs get settled, you know how they get with the hose" scolded Pat. The dogs see the hose as a great game, trying to catch the water in their mouths or dodge the water altogether. Now that Lucky is an old dog, she prefers bathing in a paddling pool with warm soapy water to revive her old joints. But always enjoys watching Starsky and Kered having fun with the hose, when Lucky was a much younger dog, she also enjoyed the same game herself. Watching them play, she felt a pang of loneliness, she did sometimes miss the company of the two dogs, especially on the rare occasions that Kaz had to leave her at home alone, but she wouldn't swap her solitude for anything these days, she had a nice comfy bed with a fleece blanket by the radiator at Kaz and Andy's house, and it wasn't often that they had to leave her home alone, usually they were able to take her with them whenever they went anywhere. But Kaz always leaves the radio on quiet for her so she doesn't get too lonely when she's left at home by herself.

"We saw somebody in the back field when we got back from our walk just now" Kaz said to her dad, "I thought it might have been you, but it obviously wasn't". "I expect it was the light playing tricks on your eyes" her dad shrugged. "No it was definitely a person" said Kaz, "we thought we'd get a takeaway for dinner" Dave said, changing the subject. Thinking nothing more of it, Kaz dried off Lucky and put the dogs into the utility room so they could settle down and dry off properly. Kered and Lucky curled up together on the large fleece blanket that Starsky normally favoured, so Starsky curled up on the old armchair feeling like the king of the castle. "Blimey I've never known Starsky give up his blanket so easily before, he must be tired out from the walk" commented Pat. "I feel so guilty having Lucky" said Kaz, noticing how inseparable Lucky and Kered have become, "don't be daft, I expect it's just because they've missed each other, she certainly seems happier in herself since she went to live with you" said Pat. "Your dad says you saw somebody in the field earlier" pat enquired, "yeah Andy saw them yesterday when we got here and we saw them again when we got back from the walk" said Kaz. Looking sad, Pat shrugged and went back inside. Thinking nothing of it,

Kaz went into the living room to decide which takeaway she fancied.

On the last day of their stay, Andy decided to walk lucky around the fields before heading back home. In the back field, Andy noticed a figure of a man at the far end, determined to find out who the person is, he started walking towards the person. Lucky immediately put her hackles up and started growling fiercely, not having a fierce bone in her body, Andy was startled by her reaction. "Don't be silly, Lucks" he said nervously. But Lucky continued to growl. As he got closer, the man, he noticed, was wearing old fashioned farming clothes with an old style trilby hat. "Hello" called Andy expecting the man to turn around, but it seemed that the man hadn't heard him, still growling, Andy called Lucky to sit and stay. "Daft dog" he muttered under his breath. Happy to oblige, Lucky immediately sat down. She didn't like the feel of this person, something didn't feel quite right but she couldn't pin point what it was. Getting nearer, Andy put his hand out to touch the man's shoulder, but his hand went straight through the man, and the man suddenly disappeared into thin air. Shocked, Andy turned to walk back to the house. Upon seeing the man disappear, Lucky barked once and immediately got up and ran back towards the house. "What's up with you two?" asked Kaz, seeing Lucky running towards her with her tail between her legs and Andy looking as white as a sheet. "You look like you've a ghost" laughed Kaz. "Nothing, it's nothing" stammered Andy, not sure how to explain what had just happened. Suddenly worried, Kaz called her dad. Andy sat on the kitchen stool while Lucky ran into the living room to be with Kered. Dave came into the kitchen wondering what all the fuss was about. Seeing Andy look so pale, he knew something had happened. "I guess my friend has let you see him" asked Dave. "What?" exclaimed Kaz, confused "He doesn't usually let himself be seen by anybody, normally just me and Pat" Dave continued. Andy explained what had just happened. "Who is he?" asked Kaz. "Pats Grandad" answered Dave. You know that this house has always been owned by Pats family?" asked Dave, nodding, Kaz and Andy waited for her dad to explain what was going on. "Well. Pats Grandad had a farming accident many years ago, before she was born, and died. While Pat was growing up she often used to see a kind, elderly gentleman in that back field, who used to talk to her and tell her stories, only nobody else could see him, so her parents used to assume she just had an imaginary friend. Until one day, Pat asked the man for his name. The man refused to give his name and his visits became less frequent. Then one day, Pats parents were sorting out some old photographs, and Pat saw a photo of the man that had been visiting her. "That's your Grandad," Pat's mum informed her. 'No, this can't be my Grandad, as my Grandad is dead. This is the man that I've been talking to in the field," Pat informed her parents. "Don't be so silly,'" her dad chastised. So Pat never mentioned the nice old man again, and the old man eventually stopped visiting. Until recently. For some reason, the old man has been visiting us again, but up to now, only myself and Pat have been the only ones able to see him, but he hasn't been talking to us, he usually just gives us a smile and wave before disappearing again. Pat is just a bit sad about it that's all" Dave said. "so that explains why you both looked at each other when Andy asked if you'd rented out that field when we got here" exclaimed Kaz, "yes, and it's also the reason why Pat isn't keen to rent out the field, even though we need the money, she's worried that he'll disappear for good if strange people are using the field" answered Dave. Feeling a mixture of shock and relief, Kaz makes a pot of tea. "Why not rent out one of the other fields instead?" Kaz asked her dad. "That's what we're probably going to do" he answered.

Packing up the car, Andy and Kaz both look over towards the field and see the same kind looking old man leaning against the gate. As Andy closes the boot, the elderly man smiles and waves and disappears. "Bye, see you next time" calls Andy into thin air.

CHRISTMAS

"Look, it's snowing," barked Starsky excitedly, nudging the door hoping to be let out to play.

"Calm down, Starsky," called Dave, his owner. "I'll let you out in a minute". Dave finished drinking his tea and started to pull on his coat and boots. Unable to curtain his excitement, Starsky started jumping about. Dave opened the door and Starsky ran out with such gusto that he skidded across the yard. "Starsky, careful" chastised Dave.

"Ruffian!" sniffed Kered from the comfort of his bed. "Kered, come" called Dave. Not liking the cold, Kered curled up in his bed into a tight ball, "KERED, COME!" called Dave again but more firm. Realising that he did in fact need to go out, Kered reluctantly got up, stretched and plodded outside. "This is fun" laughed Starsky making snow angels. Kered couldn't help but laugh at his companion as a snow flake landed on Starsky's nose. Laughing, Starsky jumped up and threw a snowball at Kered, just missing him. Scowling, Kered wandered off, wondering if Sharon would bring Tramp and his owner, Matthew over for a visit. Despite his initial reservations, Kered was very fond of Tramp, and he was turning into an amazing assistance dog for Matthew, and the pair were now almost inseparable.

"Kered, Starsky, come" called Dave from the back field. Excitedly, both dogs bounded over to the field. Despite being cold, Kered loved a game of ball. It was a game both dogs loved, seeing who could get to the ball first. Both dogs soon warmed up running around. Jumping up to catch the ball, Starsky slipped on some ice and somersaulted backwards, letting go of the ball, Kered caught it and ran back to Dave and dropped it ready for it be thrown again. Starsky brushed himself down and ran after his companion laughing. "Cheat" he said under his breath. Starsky is so foolhardy that he rarely gets hurt from his falls, and always bounces back, laughing at himself.

"Nice save" laughed Tramp running across the field to join in the fun. "TRAMP" called Starsky and Kered in excitement running across the field to greet their friend. "We didn't think you'd come because of the snow" they barked in excitement. "Guess what? We're staying for Christmas" said Tramp, equally excitable. "FANTASTC" barked Starsky & Kered high fiving and jumping up and down with excitement. Starsky & Kered loved Christmas, Tramp wasn't sure he understood what the excitement was about, but if it meant spending time with his friends, then he was happy. "Where are Matthew and Sharon?" enquired Kered. "Inside, Matthew isn't too keen on the snow and being cold" answered Tramp. After a few minutes of ball chasing, Dave called the dogs to go in. Pat and Sharon were waiting with towels to dry the dogs, and then the three of them went into the living room in companionable silence to curl up in front of the fire. "WOW! What is that?!" exclaimed Tramp at the Christmas tree and all the decorations. Forgetting that their friend hasn't had a proper Christmas. They explained about Santa Claus and the tradition of giving and receiving presents. "But how will I know it's Santa and not a burglar!?" asked Tramp. Laughing Kered answered "You'll just know". Curling up on their fleece blankets by the fire, Kered and Starsky soon fell sleep. In awe of what he had been told, Tramp curled up by Matthews' feet, but was too excited to sleep, wondering what the next day would bring.

The next morning, the three dogs were awoken early by delighted yells coming from the living room. Starsky and Kered yawned and stretched, knowing that the excitement was Matthew having discovered that Santa had been in the night and placed lots of gifts under the tree. "What time is it" yawned Tramp, realising that it was still dark. Sharon came through to the kitchen and switched on the kettle, and opened the back door to let the dogs outside. "Wow it's snowed again in the night" noticed Tramp, seeing the fresh untouched snow in the yard. Running about in excitement, Starsky caught a snowflake on his tongue.

Laughing, the three dogs jumped and skidded about in excitement. "Come on you lot" called Pat, leading the dogs to the field with a ball, to give the dogs a quick game before breakfast.

After a quick dry off and breakfast, the dogs went into the living room. All three dogs were in awe of the huge pile of presents that were under the tree. Matthew, still in his pyjama's was jumping up and down, clapping his hands with excitement at all the brightly wrapped objects. "But I never heard Santa come in" said Tramp, concerned that his guarding abilities had let him down the night before. "Santa is magic, that's why we never heard him" Starsky informed his friend. "Wow" Tramp exclaimed. In complete awe at what he saw.

Unable to curtain his excitement any longer, Matthew started to open his presents, lots of toys and games soon began to litter the floor. It was some time before Starsky and Kered realised that their friend was no longer with them. Going out to investigate, Kered found Tramp Curled up in his bed looking sad. "Why the sad face?" asked Kered. "Now that Matthew has so many new things, he won't need me now, I'll have to go back to the beach to live," sobbed Tramp. Shocked by what they heard, Starsky and Kered reassured their friend that Matthew did indeed still need Tramp around to maintain his independence. Matthew had become so much more confident since Tramp came into his life; the two dogs knew that Tramp was Matthew's best friend in the whole world. "Come on" said Kered, "There's normally a present or two for us if we're lucky" excitedly, Starsky and Kered went back into the living room hoping for their presents to be opened soon. Tramp stayed in the kitchen, working out how he could slip out un-noticed, the thought of leaving Matthew tore his heart in two, but it was obvious to him that the child wasn't interested in him now he had so many new things to play with.

After a while, Pat went into the kitchen to start cooking dinner. Feeling cold, she saw that the back door was slightly open. Closing it, she set about making Christmas dinner, smiling as she heard lots of happy sounds coming from the living room. While she was chopping carrots Dave walked in with all the dog treats to put away, "Where's Tramp?" asked Dave. "Matthew wants to give him his special present but he's not in the living room". "I don't know, come to think of it, I haven't noticed him for quite a while, what with all the excitement of watching Matthew, I haven't paid much attention to the dogs, I just assumed they'd all be together in there" Pat answered. "He's bound to be here somewhere, maybe all the noise Matthew was making spooked him a bit, and He's prob just gone for a bit of peace and quiet" Dave shrugged.

By the time dinner was ready, Tramp still hadn't appeared and Matthew was starting to get agitated. Wondering where he could have gone, Pat remembered that the back door was open slightly when she first went into the kitchen so put on her coat and boots and called Starsky and Kered to go and look for him outside. "He can't have gone far, maybe he just needed to go out and couldn't get back in because I'd closed the door" said Pat. "We'll soon find him" she tried to reassure Matthew, who was now quite upset that his best friend had disappeared.

Realising what had happened, Starsky and Kered knew they had to find Tramp as soon as possible. Pat walked towards the back field hoping he'd be there, knowing that Tramp had likely gone back to the beach, Starsky and Kered knew they had to get Pat to follow them there. Barking to attract Pat's attention, Starsky and Kered ran to the gate barking frantically. "What is up with you pair" called Pat, walking towards the gate, maybe they had seen Tramp. So she opened the gate, and they ran down the road, stopped, turned and barked and ran off again hoping to get Pat to follow. "Starsky, Kered, Come NOW" called Pat. Wondering what on earth was wrong with the two dogs. They'd never done anything like this before. Carrying on with their plan of running, stopping and barking, Pat did start to follow the dogs. Eventually, they arrived at the beach and Starsky and Kered ran to where Tramp used to sleep, hoping that he'd have gone back to the same place. Running after the dogs Pat wondered what had got into them.

Starsky and Kered found Tramp huddled up into a tight ball fast asleep. Sighing with relief, they shook him awake. Pat caught up with the dogs and was shocked and amazed by what she saw, how on earth did they know where to find Tramp! Pat was so shocked by the intelligence of her dogs; she stood still taking it all in. Surprised to see his friends, Tramp jumped up "how did you find me" he asked. "Duh! We knew straight away that this is where you'd be," chastised Kered. "Matthew is frantic, you have to come back," Starsky told Tramp. "No, you saw how he was, he doesn't want me now," said Tramp so forlornly. Kered told his friend how upset Matthew was when he went to give his best friend his present but couldn't find him. We had to think of something to get Pat to follow us, as we knew that we'd find you here. Looking up, he saw Pat nearby talking on her mobile phone. "I've been very silly, haven't I?" said Tramp. "Yep," grinned Starsky. "Come on; let's go home, you have a huge present to open from a very special person". Slipping leads onto the three dogs Pat walked back to the road where Dave was waiting for them in his car.

When they returned home, Matthew ran to the car with such excitement and cuddled Tramp as tight as he could, relieved that he had been found. Following

Matthew into the house, Starsky and Kered sat in front of the fire while Tramp tried on his brand new coat collar and lead that Matthew had brought for him.

"I'm amazed how they knew where to find him," Pat said to Sharon when she asked where he was. "I thought they were being disobedient but they knew all along where he was," Pat answered stroking Kered's ear.

After dinner, Starsky and Kered curled up in front of the fire happy and contented while Tramp curled up by Matthew's feet and vowed that he would never doubt his best friends ever again.